LEVEL 2 READER

POKÉMON JOURNEYS THE SERIES

MYSTERY OF THE MISSING FOOD

Adapted by Maria S. Barbo

©2022 Pokémon. ©1997–2020 Nintendo, Creatures, GAME FREAK, TV Tokyo, ShoPro, JR Kikaku. TM, ® Nintendo.

All rights reserved. Published by Scholastic Inc., *Publishers since 1920*. SCHOLASTIC and associated logos are trademarks and/or registered trademarks of Scholastic Inc.

The publisher does not have any control over and does not assume any responsibility for author or third-party websites or their content.

No part of this publication may be reproduced, stored in a retrieval system, or transmitted in any form or by any means, electronic, mechanical, photocopying, recording, or otherwise, without written permission of the publisher. For information regarding permission, write to Scholastic Inc., Attention: Permissions Department, 557 Broadway, New York, NY 10012.

This book is a work of fiction. Names, characters, places, and incidents are either the product of the author's imagination or are used fictitiously, and any resemblance to actual persons, living or dead, business establishments, events, or locales is entirely coincidental.

ISBN 978-1-338-84809-0

10 9 8 7 6 5 4 3 2   22 23 24 25 26

Designed by Cheung Tai

Printed in the U.S.A.   40

First printing 2022

SCHOLASTIC INC.

"Beedrill! Beedrill!" buzzed Beedrill.
"Grimer," moaned Grimer.
"Skwovet?" asked Skwovet.
Ash's and Goh's Pokémon were hungry.

Hungry Pokémon became grumpy Pokémon.

Grumpy Pokémon started to fight.

"I don't get it," said Goh. "We just fed them."
Ash and Goh watched from their computer.
The food was already gone.

"One of them must be stealing all the food!" said Goh.

They decided to sleep in Cerise Park to catch the thief.

Pikachu liked that plan.

Ash and Goh set up camp in the park.
They brought food to use as bait.
They took turns watching.

"Don't let your guard down," said Goh.
"You can count on me!" said Ash.
Pikachu snuggled next to Ash.

The next morning, Ash and Pikachu
woke up with a Thunderbolt.

"Pika! Pika!" cried Pikachu.

They had fallen asleep!

All the Pokémon food was gone!

But they didn't have time to think about it.

The hungry Pokémon were ready to rumble.

Darmanitan pounded its belly.
It blasted the Bug types with a ring of fire.
Scyther blocked the move.

All the Bug-type Pokémon charged.
"I can't just stand here and watch!" shouted Ash.

"Pikachu! Riolu!" called Ash.
"Shut it down now!"
"Help them out, Raboot!" said Goh.
Pikachu, Riolu, and Raboot dove in.

One by one, they got the boot.
"We can't stop the fighting," said Goh.
Ash called on Dragonite to help.
Dragonite wanted to let the Pokémon
work out their own problems.

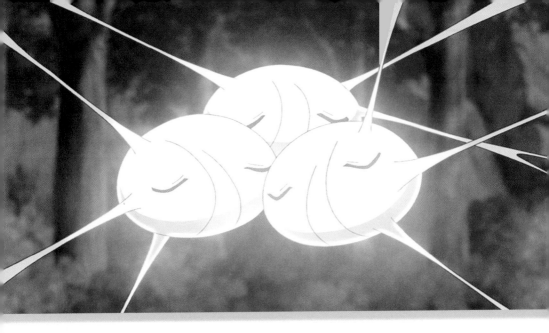

"Check out the Cascoon!" Goh shouted.
The Bug-type Pokémon glowed pink.
They were trying to evolve!
But a stray fireball from the fight
was heading straight for them.

"This is bad!" shouted Goh.

Ash reached for a Poké Ball.

But Golurk was faster.

The giant Pokémon stepped in front of the Cascoon.

Its body blocked the blast!

A metal plate fell off Golurk's chest.
A red beam shot up into the sky.
Black clouds rushed in.
Rain fell down.

Golurk slammed its fist into the ground.
"Golurk can't control its energy!" Ash cried.

Pikachu leaped into action.
Raboot and Riolu followed.
Pidgey and Farfetch'd flew in to patch Golurk's chest.
Skwovet and Cubone climbed up to help.
Their plan was working!
Golurk was back to normal.
But the storm kept raging!

A giant wave of water rushed at the Cascoon's tree.
"If this keeps up, they might not evolve," said Ash.
Golurk and Dragonite held the tree steady.
Pikachu, Riolu, and Raboot called to the other
Pokémon.
The Pokémon stopped fighting and got to work.

Darmanitan dashed in with the Bug-type
Pokémon.

Scyther rallied the Water-type Pokémon.

Grimer led the Ground types and Poison types.

"Everyone's working together!" said Ash.

"Wow," said Goh. "All so the Cascoon can evolve."

Ash and Goh watched as the Cascoon evolved into Dustox.

The Dustox swirled into the sky.

The rain stopped.

The clouds melted away.

The sky turned a bright, clear blue.

The next morning, the Pokémon ate together.
No one fought.
"We still haven't solved the mystery," said Goh.

"Who took all the food?"

BONK!

A pile of pellets fell on the Trainers' heads.

Ash and Goh followed the trail of treats.
They found a small cave.
It was packed with Pokémon food!
"Skwovet!"

A small, furry Pokémon blasted more food into the cave.

Ash shook his head. "Why?"

"Wait!" said Goh.

"Hiding food is what Skwovet do!"

Ash and Goh laughed.

They decided to bring extra food for Skwovet to store.

With that, peace returned to Cerise Park.